Carla Carlita Explodes

Illustrated by Ron Florendo

By Nicole Rondeau

Monday morning, as Carla Carlita was getting ready for school, she heard her mother shout, "Carla, why don't you wear your red dress today?!" Her mother shouted every day, and every day, Carla wore what her mother wanted, but not today!

Today, Carla was going to choose what she wanted to wear, and it certainly was not the red dress!

"Hmmm, what to wear..." Carla asked herself. She wasn't used to making her own decisions. It was hard.

"The blue dress...no," she said as she flung the dress onto her bed. "The purple pants...the pink shorts...the orange skirt...no! No! No!"

The pile of clothes on the bed got higher and higher. "Hmmm, the pink pants or the yellow and pink dress? I can't decide, so I'll wear both!" She quickly got dressed and brushed out her long brown hair.

"Hmm, what colour hair ties should I put into my pigtails?" she asked herself. "Should I wear the pink bows or the yellow ones? I can't decide, so I'll wear one of each!" And she did.

As Carla was walking out the door, she turned and looked at her bedroom. Oh no, what a mess! She quickly picked up all the clothes from her bed and threw them into the closet. She shut the door and hurried off to school to show her friends her cool outfit.

The school bus pulled up in front of the school. Carla was the first one to scurry through the big yellow doors and skip into the schoolyard. There, she found her three best friends.

"Neat outfit!" said Jessica.
"Wow, cool clothes!" said Shelby.
"Awesome!" said Josie.

Carla was beaming with pride. "I picked it out by myself!" She twirled around fourteen times to be sure they saw how pretty she looked. By the time she stopped twirling, she was dizzy. From now on, she would make all of her decisions! After all, she knew best!

The next morning as Carla was rolling out of bed, she heard her mother shout, "Why don't you wear your purple dress with the matching purple socks, honey?"

"Purple, shmurple," said Carla. "I'm six years old. I can make my own decisions." With that, Carla started flinging clothes from the bottom of her closet where she had left them the morning before.

"Pink jumper...no. Yellow dress...no. Blue pants...no." She tossed everything onto her bed. Finally, she chose several things. She couldn't decide which ones to wear, so she wore them all. She put on her favourite blue dress with white dots, pink pants, a pair of yellow shorts, a purple jumper, and purple socks to please her mother.

Now she would have to find the hair ties to match! She wore two big blue bows, white barrettes, small yellow hair clips, and her favourite pink hat on top of it all.

She looked into the mirror and saw that she looked quite stunning. "Wait until I show my friends!"

She looked at her room as though for the first time and saw the pile of clothes two feet high on her bed. She scooped everything up into her arms and threw it all into the bottom of the closet.

This decision-making sure took a lot of time. She had to hurry or she would miss her bus.

"You really should eat your breakfast, dear," said her mother as Carla was putting on her shoes. Her mother was looking at her strangely.

"I've decided I don't really need breakfast," said Carla. "Besides, I don't have time." And she ran out the door.

Jessica, Josie, and Shelby were all waiting for Carla to get off the bus. When she finally did, they all oohed and aahed! They loved her cool clothes! She twirled and twirled and twirled around in circles thirty-four times and finally landed on her bottom. She was dizzy and weak. After all, she hadn't had breakfast. That was okay; she would eat her lunch at recess. And she did.

When Carla woke up Wednesday morning, she was very tired! She opened her heavy eyelids and looked at her closet. *Oh no, not this again! Decisions, decisions...what to wear?*

Just then, she heard her mother shout, "How about wearing the lovely skirt your Uncle Kamilo sent you for Christmas?"

"Kamilo, hamilo," muttered Carla. Not today. Today she was going to wear something really different.

Carla started to look through the clothes piled high in the bottom of her closet. "Hmmm...things are getting pretty crushed and wrinkled. Maybe it's time to check the dresser drawers," she decided.

She opened her drawers and discovered many more pants and many more sweaters! Oh no, more clothes to choose from! She began pulling out pair after pair of pants. Yellow ones, green ones, striped ones, purple ones, orange ones, and spotted ones. She threw them all on her bed and picked out four of her favourite pairs.

Now, she would need a sweater to wear with this. She tossed out sweater after sweater. There were sweaters of every style and colour! Pink ones, red ones, dotted ones, long-sleeved ones, short-sleeved ones. Hundreds and hundreds of them! She finally chose four pretty ones to match the four pairs of pants she had picked out.

Carla Carlita could not decide which outfit to wear,
so she wore them all!

To please her mother, she decided to wear her new skirt on top of her four pairs of pants along with her four matching sweaters.

Once again, Carla was running out of time. Her bus would soon be here, and she still had to choose her hair ties. She quickly looked through her big box of hair accessories and began frantically clipping bows here, tying ribbons there, and snapping barrettes here, there, and everywhere. Finally she was ready for school.

She looked at her bed. Pants and sweaters were stacked four feet high. She scooped it all up and threw it into the closet with all the other clothes. The pile of clothing reached the ceiling! She closed the door and ran downstairs.

Carla ran to the front door and slipped on her shoes. Luckily, she only had one pair of shoes. She wouldn't have to decide which ones to wear.

Her mother called out to her, "Carla, you forgot your lunch and you didn't eat breakfast!"

"I'll figure something out," she shouted as she ran out the door and to the bus.

Shelby, Jessica, and Josie stood staring as Carla got off the bus. Carla had changed. She looked...thicker. She had different colours of clothing sticking out of her sleeves and her pant legs and her skirt didn't match.
She had so many hair things in her hair that her head was lopsided.
And then she started to spin.

Carla twirled and twirled fifty-two times so that her friends could see how pretty she looked. She finally stopped and fell on her face. She was dizzy and hungry! She would have to wait until lunch to eat.

When lunch time rolled around, Carla and her friends sat together in the school's cafeteria. Shelby, Jessica, and Josie were nice enough to share their lunch with Carla.

Carla Carlita had trouble eating. Her clothes were too tight, and she was very hot. As she ate, her clothes got tighter and tighter, and she got hotter and hotter. She stood up to be more comfortable. Suddenly, the buttons on her skirt flew off, her skirt fell down, and all the children in the cafeteria began laughing hysterically!

Some of the children were shouting, "Carla lost her skirt! Carla lost her skirt!" Carla Carlita's face turned seventeen shades of red. Luckily, she had four pairs of pants under her skirt.

Friday morning, Carla Carlita's mother had to shake Carla to wake her up.

Carla opened her eyes. She looked at her mother. She looked at her closet. She put her head under the covers.

"Carla, sweetheart," said her mother, "why don't you just wear the really pretty green pants with the little brown belt. They look so nice on you." She went downstairs to prepare breakfast.

"Green pants, purple ants, silly plants," said Carla. "I know exactly what I'm going to wear today." But she didn't.

Carla Carlita opened all of her drawers. They were all empty. She looked at the closet. She had no choice. She tried to slide open the closet door. It was stuck. She pushed and she pulled and she pushed and she pulled eighteen times before the door finally flew off of the track and fell onto the floor.

Carla looked up at the mountain of clothes. She began to tug and pull at some of her dresses when the entire pile fell over her. She was buried under her clothes. She had to claw and drag herself out from underneath.

Just then, her mother shouted,
"Carla, hurry! Your bus will be here soon!"

Carla wasn't even dressed yet! Quickly, she pulled on some of her prettiest outfits. She pulled up pants, yanked down sweaters, slipped on dresses, and pulled on skirts.

Just when she thought she was almost ready, her mother called out to her, "Put on a warm sweater, dear. It's chilly out!"

Oh my goodness, oh my frogness! Which sweater will I wear?
My pink one or my striped one? She couldn't decide, so she wore them both. Then, she decided to make her mother happy, and she tried to put on her brown belt. It was too tight with all those clothes. She tugged and she pulled and she tugged and she pulled until she was finally able to buckle it at the very last notch.

Carla raced to her hair thing box and snapped, clipped, and tied ribbons, bows, and barrettes all over her long, brown, tangled hair. She hadn't had time to comb it.

Finally, she was ready. She looked at the chaos in her room. It would have to wait until after school. She ran out the door to catch her bus. It wasn't until she was on the bus, that she realized she hadn't had breakfast, she didn't have her lunch, and she had forgotten to put on her shoes!

This decision-making was becoming more and more difficult.

When the bus stopped in front of the school, Carla Carlita tried to get out of her seat, but she couldn't. She was stuck! She had so many clothes on that she was squished tightly in the seat. Two boys who were sitting across from her grabbed both of her hands and yanked her out. She jerked out of her seat, flew through the open door, and rolled all the way to the schoolyard. Luckily, she had lots of clothes on so she didn't even get a scratch.

Shelby, Jessica, and Josie helped Carla to her feet. They stared at her with their mouths hanging wide open and their eyes bulging out of their heads. What had Carla done?

Then she began to twirl. She twirled and twirled and twirled so fast, she couldn't stop. She crashed into seven girls playing hop scotch. The little girls flew all over the schoolyard. She smashed into ten small boys playing with marbles. They were tossed every which way.

They were all screaming, but Carla didn't hear them, she was spinning so fast! Finally, she spun right into the wall of the school and came to a stop. The school bell rang. Carla was so dizzy she could hardly get to her class!

"For your homework last night, I asked you children to prepare a short story," said Miss Evelsnotter, their first grade teacher. "Carla, could you please stand in front of the class to read yours?"

Carla was still dizzy. She waddled like a stuffed turkey to the front of the classroom. She started to read her story, but she had trouble concentrating. She was very hot, and she could feel her face turning red. As Carla was reading, the top buttons of her sweater popped off and hit the boy in the second row.

He screamed, "Look out! Carla's going to explode!" And she did.

Carla's belt blew apart, buttons popped off, snaps sailed through the air, clasps and zippers pelted the little children, and bows and barrettes popped like popcorn. The classroom was covered with Carla's clothes. The children were laughing and screaming, but Carla felt much better. She knew what she had to do.

When Carla got home, she folded all of her clothes and put them neatly away where they belonged. It took her all weekend. She was exhausted, but that night, she slept better than she had all week.

Monday morning, Carla heard her mother shout, "Sweetie, would you please wear the little flowered dress you got for Easter?"

Carla shouted back, "I will wear the flowered dress today, if I can wear the purple spotted one tomorrow!"

"Sure," said her mother.

Carla had learned to compromise. This way, Carla was happy, her mother was happy, and her closet was much neater.

Photo courtesy of Alicia Drinkwalter

Nicole lives in Brandon, Manitoba, with her husband and four children. She began storytelling as a child, entertaining her siblings and cousins at a young age. She started writing when her children were small, drawing from their hilarious antics; they are her inspiration, and continue to be. She enjoys their laughter and loves to dote on her grandchild. Because of her husband's career, they spent many years moving throughout the country. Today she has a very successful business relocating seniors and also working for a major newspaper.